To Alex and Marco, the two clever foxes next door,
and to jkandsr with thanks - SM

First Edition 2006
Paperback Edition 2006
Spanish Language Hardcover Edition 2006
Spanish Language Paperback Edition 2006

HOOPOE

Published by Hoopoe Books,
a division of The Institute for the Study of Human Knowledge

Visit www.hoopoekids.com for a complete list of
Hoopoe titles, CDs, DVDs, an introduction on the
use of Teaching-Stories™ *Learning that Lasts*,
and parent/teacher guides.

ISBN:1-883536-43-X

Library of Congress Cataloging-in-Publication Data

Shah, Idries, 1924-.
 The man and the fox / by Idries Shah.-- 1st ed.
   p. cm.
 Summary: Relates how a clever fox outwits the man who set a trap for him by promising him a chicken.
 ISBN 1-883536-43-X (hardcover)
[1. Folklore. 2. Foxes--Folklore.] 1. Title.

PZ8.1 .S47 Mal 2006
398.24'529775--dc22

2005031628

THE MAN AND THE FOX

by
Idries Shah

HOOPOE BOOKS

BOSTON

ONCE UPON A TIME, when the moon grew on a tree and ants were fond of pickles, there was a lovely brown fox.

 He had soft fur,
beautiful whiskers,

and a fine,
bushy tail.

This fox, whose name was Rowba, was sitting beside a road one day, combing his whiskers with his claws, when a man came along.

"May you never be tired!" said the man.

"May you always be happy!" replied Rowba.

"I'm feeling generous today," said the man. "Is there anything you would like?"

"I would like a chicken," said Rowba, because foxes love to eat chickens.

"Come along with me, then, and I'll give you one!" replied the man. "I have chickens at my house. We'll go there, and you'll have your chicken in no time at all."

"How marvelous!" said Rowba.

And he trotted down the road beside the man.

When they got to the man's house, the man said, "Wait outside. I'll go to the yard in the back and get you one of my birds."

So Rowba sat down to wait and
the man went into his house.

Then the man took a sack and put some
stones into it. You see, he was going to
pretend there was a chicken in the sack.
He wasn't really going to give
a chicken to the fox at all!

When the man came out again, he handed Rowba the sack and said, "Here you are, there's a chicken in this sack."

"How wonderful!" said Rowba, and he was just about to open the sack to eat the chicken when the man said:

"No! Don't open it here!"

"Why not?" asked Rowba.

"Well," said the man, "the farmers around here can see us, and they won't like my giving a chicken to a fox."

Of course, that wasn't true at all. The man just didn't want the fox to see that there were only stones in the sack.

"What shall I do, then?" asked Rowba.

"Do you see those bushes up there?" asked the man, pointing. "Take the sack there and open it. Nobody will see you, and you can eat your chicken in peace."

"That's a good idea," said Rowba. "Thank you very much!"

And he trotted all the way to the bushes carrying the sack in his mouth.

As soon as Rowba crawled under the bushes,
he opened the sack and saw the stones inside.

"Strange!" he muttered to himself.
"What kind of a funny joke is this?"

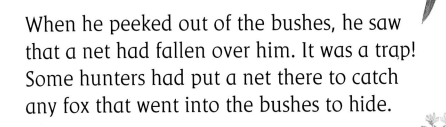

When he peeked out of the bushes, he saw
that a net had fallen over him. It was a trap!
Some hunters had put a net there to catch
any fox that went into the bushes to hide.

At first Rowba was worried because he thought he might not get out of the net. But he was very clever.

Foxes are very, very clever, you know.
He searched through the stones in the
sack and found one with a sharp edge.
With this, he began to cut the net.

He cut a hole big enough for his left
front paw to fit through.

He cut some more, and soon the hole was big enough
for his left and his right front paws to fit through.

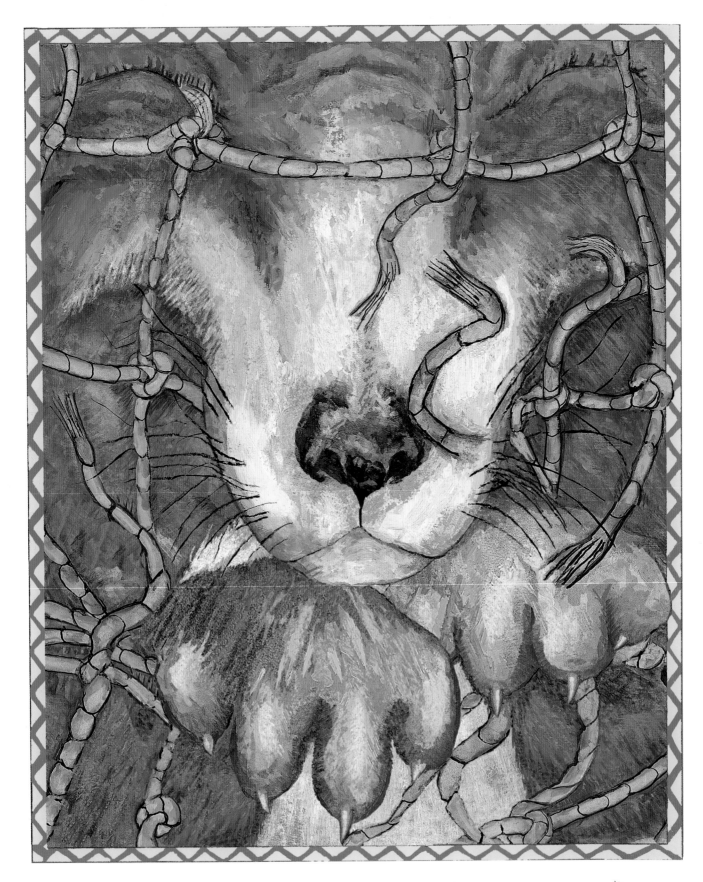

 He cut still more, and soon the hole was big enough for his two front paws and his nose to fit through.

He kept on cutting, and soon
the hole was big enough for his front paws,
his nose and the rest of his head to fit through.

Then he pushed and wiggled
just a bit more. And finally ...

Rowba escaped!

As Rowba ran off down the road, he laughed and laughed and laughed.

"Men may think they are clever," he said to himself, "but foxes are cleverer still!"

Now, all foxes know the story of Rowba and the man who promised him a chicken. And that is the reason why, whenever you see a fox, if you ask him to come for a walk with you, he won't.

And that is why it is very, very difficult to catch foxes and why they live such a free and happy life.

Other Books by Idries Shah

For Young Readers

The Boy Without a Name
The Clever Boy and the Terrible, Dangerous Animal
The Farmer's Wife
Fatima The Spinner and the Tent
The Lion Who Saw Himself in the Water
The Magic Horse
The Man with Bad Manners
Neem the Half-Boy
The Old Woman and the Eagle
The Silly Chicken
World Tales

Literature
The Hundred Tales of Wisdom
A Perfumed Scorpion
Caravan of Dreams
Wisdom of the Idiots
The Magic Monastery
The Dermis Probe

Novel
Kara Kush

Informal Beliefs
Oriental Magic
The Secret Lore of Magic

Humor
The Exploits of the Incomparable Mulla Nasrudin
The Pleasantries of the Incredible Mulla Nasrudin
The Subtleties of the Inimitable Mulla Nasrudin
The World of Nasrudin
Special Illumination

Human Thought
Learning How to Learn
The Elephant in the Dark
Thinkers of the East
Reflections
A Veiled Gazelle
Seeker After Truth

Sufi Studies
The Sufis
The Way of the Sufi
Tales of the Dervishes
The Book of the Book
Neglected Aspects of Sufi Study
The Commanding Self
Knowing How to Know

Studies of the English
Darkest England
The Natives are Restless
The Englishman's Handbook